BEYOND THE MILKY WAY

WRITTEN AND ILLUSTRATED BY
CECILE SCHOBERLE

CROWN PUBLISHERS, INC.   NEW YORK

Copyright © 1986 by Cecile Schoberle

All rights reserved. No part of this book may be reproduced
or transmitted in any form or by any means,
electronic or mechanical, including photocopying, recording,
or by any information storage and retrieval system,
without permission in writing from the publisher.
Published by Crown Publishers, Inc., 225 Park Avenue South, New York, New York 10003
Manufactured in the Netherlands
CROWN is a trademark of Crown Publishers, Inc.

Library of Congress Cataloging in Publication Data
Schoberle, Cecile.   Beyond the Milky Way.
Summary: Looking out a city window and seeing
the night sky between the buildings, a child describes
the glowing wonder of outer space and imagines another
child doing the same on a distant planet.
[1. Outer space—Fiction] I. Title.
PZ7.S3647Be 1986   [E]   85-11661
ISBN 0-517-55716-9
10 9 8 7 6 5 4 3 2 1
First Edition

Dedicated to Stephen G. Walsh.

Out of my window,

I can see between the buildings.

Between the buildings, I can see
the twilight blue of the summer sky.

In the sky, I can see the lights from an airplane blinking…off…and on.

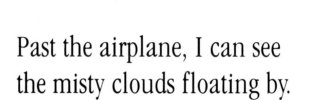

Past the airplane, I can see
the misty clouds floating by.

Above the clouds,
I can see the
diamond-bright
stars and
the swirling
Milky Way.

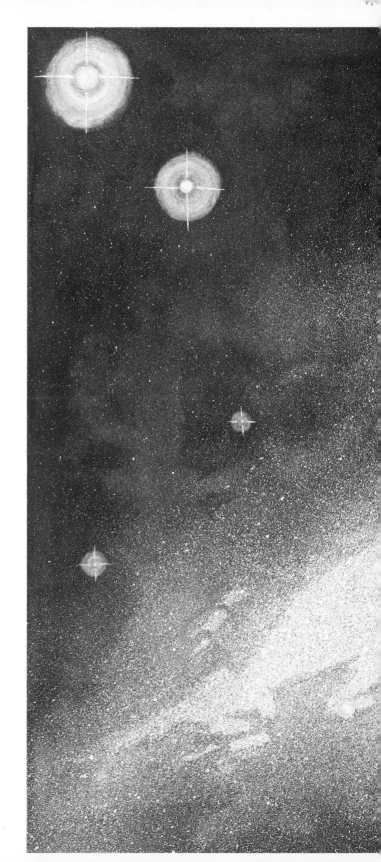

Beyond the Milky Way, I can imagine
the glowing planets.

On a planet,

I wonder if there's someone else
who can see between her buildings.

Between the buildings, maybe she can see
the velvet blue of her summer sky.

In the sky, perhaps she can see
the spaceship lights flashing…
off…and on.

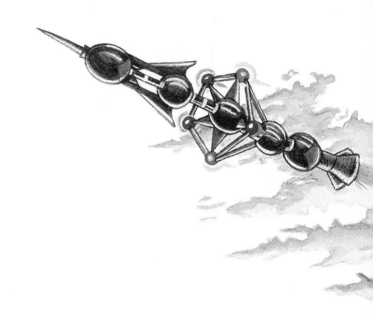

Past the spaceship, maybe she can see
the feathery clouds drifting by.

Above the clouds,
maybe she can see
the crystal-clear stars
and the flowing
Milky Way.

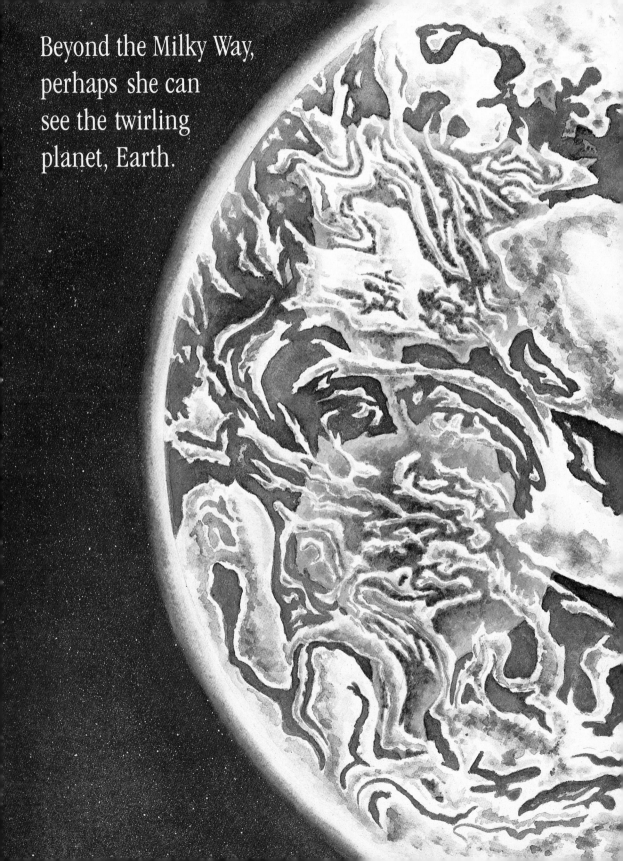

Beyond the Milky Way,
perhaps she can
see the twirling
planet, Earth.

And does she wonder if I am here
on Earth, looking out my window?